Happy Pig Day!

To Hilary Price,
who celebrates everyone

ISBN 978-1-338-11333-4

Text and illustrations copyright © 2011 by Mo Willems. All rights reserved.
Published by Scholastic Inc., 557 Broadway, New York, NY 10012, by arrangement
with Hyperion Books for Children, an imprint of Disney Book Group.
SCHOLASTIC and associated logos are trademarks and/or registered
trademarks of Scholastic Inc.

12 11 10 9 8 7 6 5 4 3   17 18 19 20 21

Printed in the U.S.A.   40

First Scholastic printing, September 2016

Gerald!

Gerald!

Today is the *best* day of the year!

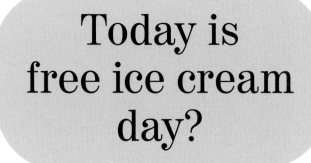

HAPPY
PIG
DAY!

8

Happy Pig Day?

14

It is the best day
to play pig games!

23

Isn't this
great, Gerald?

Gerald?

34

36

47

Happy Pig Day is for . . .

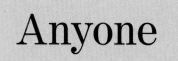

51

57

Have you read all of Elephant and Piggie's funny adventures?